BY HARPER PARIS • ILLUSTRATED BY MARCOS CALO

LITTLE SIMON
New York London Toronto Sydney New Delhi

LITTLE SIMON
An imprint of Simon & Schuster Children's Publishing Division • 1230 Avenue of the Americas, New York, New York 10020 • For information about special discounts for bulk purchases, please contact Simon & Schuster Special Sales at 1-866-506-1949 or business@simonandschuster.com. The Simon & Schuster Speakers Bureau can bring authors to your live event. For more information or to book an event contact the Simon & Schuster Speakers Bureau at 1-866-248-3049 or visit our website at www.simonspeakers.com.
Designed by John Daly. Manufactured in the United States of America 1213 FFG
First Edition 10 9 8 7 6 5 4 3 2 1
Library of Congress Cataloging-in-Publication Data
Paris, Harper. The mystery of the mosaic / by Harper Paris ; illustrated by Marcos Calo. — First edition. pages cm. — (Greetings from somewhere ; #2) Summary: In Venice, Italy, second graders Ethan and Ella hope to find a stolen gondola and a hidden mosaic before their parents realize they are missing. [1. Brothers and sisters—Fiction. 2. Twins—Fiction. 3. Venice (Italy)—Fiction. 4. Italy—Fiction. 5. Mystery and detective stories.] I. Calo, Marcos, illustrator. II. Title. PZ7.P21748Myw 2014 [E]—dc23 2013013012
ISBN 978-1-4424-9721-4 (pbk)
ISBN 978-1-4424-9722-1 (hc)
ISBN 978-1-4424-9723-8 (eBook)

TABLE OF CONTENTS

The Floating City

Ella Briar and her twin brother, Ethan, had never been to Venice, Italy, before. They'd never been to a floating city, either!

Venice was made up of a bunch of tiny islands connected by canals and bridges. The canals were like streets, except filled with water. So

some people were using boats to get around, and others were walking over the bridges from one little street to another!

The Briar family had traveled by water taxi from the airport. The sleek motorboat pulled up to a cream-colored building with lots of balconies.

"Here's our hotel!" the twins' mother, Josephine Briar, said brightly.

PENSIONE MISTERO
3

Their dad, Andrew, pushed his glasses up on his nose and pointed to his guidebook. "It says here that the Pensione Mistero is one of the oldest hotels in Venice."

"Is it older than you *guys*?" Ella asked with a sneaky smile.

Mr. Briar laughed. "I should hope so. It was built more than eight hundred years ago."

The four of them stepped out of the boat with their suitcases. Pink, yellow, and pale green buildings lined both sides of the canal. Pretty flowers and vines filled the window boxes. There

were no cars or bicycles on the cobble-stone streets, only people walking.

For a moment, Ella and Ethan were so awed by their surroundings that they forgot they were supposed to be sad. Or mad. Or sad *and* mad.

Just yesterday, they had said good-bye to everything and everyone they loved: their house in Brookeston, their friends, their school, and most of all, their Grandpa Harry. Their

mom was starting her new job as a travel writer. That meant she had to travel to different foreign cities and write about them for her newspaper column, Journeys with Jo!

It also meant the rest of the family had to travel with her. Ella and Ethan had *not* been happy about that. While Mrs. Briar was out researching and writing, Mr. Briar would be homeschooling the twins.

When the Briars entered the hotel, a woman greeted them from the front desk.

"*Buon giorno!* Hello! I am Sofia," she said cheerfully. She handed the Briars a large gold key and told them their rooms were on the fourth floor.

There was no elevator, so the family climbed up the narrow, twisting staircase. When they got to their door, they found an orange cat in the hallway! It wore a leather collar with a silver bell on it.

"Hi. Who are you?" Ella smiled and bent down to look at it. It purred and rubbed against her leg.

"It probably doesn't understand English," Ethan said. "You should speak Italian."

"I'm sure this kitty doesn't care what language you speak as long as you pet it," Mrs. Briar joked.

"I'm going to call you 'Pumpkin'

because you look like a cute little pumpkin," Ella told the cat.

Pumpkin meowed.

The Briars went inside using the gold key, and Pumpkin followed. The living room had tall ceilings, antique furniture, and a view of the canal.

There were two bedrooms and a small kitchen too.

Ella thought about her room back in Brookeston. She thought about her seashell and shark tooth collections.

She thought about Grandma Lucy's old desk, where she wrote her poems and short stories. She thought about the tree house in the backyard.

Then she tried to push all those thoughts out of her mind. *This* was their new home now—well, at least for the next few weeks it was. She and Ethan would just have to make the most of it.

The Two Hawks

"I think our restaurant is right around the next corner," Mr. Briar said, squinting at a map of Venice.

It was dinnertime, and the Briars were headed to a place called the Marco Polo Ristorante. Grandpa Harry had recommended it to them.

Ethan and Ella followed their dad along a crowded street lined with shops and cafés. Their mom trailed after them in her high-heeled shoes. She was talking to someone on her cell phone about the Doge's Palace.

"Hey, Dad? What is the Doge's Palace?" Ella asked.

"A long time ago, Venice was ruled by someone called a 'doge.' A doge was elected by the people of Venice to lead the city for his entire lifetime. Now the palace is a sight for visitors like us." Mr. Briar was a history professor and knew interesting stuff like that.

A few minutes later, they reached the Marco Polo Ristorante. Inside, the air smelled yummy, like garlic and tomato sauce. Black-and-white photographs and

flickering candles lined the brick walls.

"Why are lots of places in Venice named Marco Polo something?" Ethan wondered out loud. He remembered that the airport was called the Marco Polo Airport. He also remembered seeing a sign for the Hotel Marco Polo. Marco Polo was his absolute favorite

swimming pool game, too!

"Marco Polo was a famous explorer. He was born in Venice," Mr. Briar explained.

A tall man in a tuxedo came up to them. "*Buona sera!* Good evening! Do you have a reservation?"

"We do!" Mrs. Briar said, closing her cell phone. "Briar, table for four. My father, Harry Robinson, used to come to your restaurant a long time ago," she told the man.

"Of course! Signor Robinson is a dear friend," the man said affectionately. "My name is Luigi. Please, come right this way."

Luigi led them to a table overlooking

the canal. Ella thought the water looked beautiful at night. Ethan peered out the window. Outside, there was an old stone bridge with a dock underneath. There was a long black and green boat tied to the dock. Ethan admired it through the glass. He noticed a small gold ornament on the front of it, but from his angle, he couldn't quite make out what it was.

Luigi saw Ethan looking at the boat. "That boat is called a gondola. It belongs to my son, Antonio," he explained. "It has been in our family for many generations. *Antonio!*"

A young man with curly dark hair rushed over to their table with menus.

"Antonio, this is the family of my friend Harry Robinson—the one from America," Luigi told his son.

Antonio's eyes widened. "Oh! This is a very great honor!"

Ella leaned toward Ethan. "They must *really* like Grandpa Harry," she whispered.

Ethan nodded. Grandpa Harry was a famous archaeologist. Archaeologists studied people

from the ancient past by looking at the things they left behind, such as artwork and old buildings. Like Marco Polo, Grandpa Harry once traveled around the world exploring for his work.

Grandpa Harry must have met Luigi

and Antonio on one of his trips, Ethan thought.

Antonio started to hand the Briars their menus. But his father grabbed them and clutched them to his chest. "No menus! I will prepare a special meal just for you," Luigi announced to the Briars. "A little mozzarella, maybe some pasta à la carbonara . . ." He turned and rushed off to the kitchen.

"Mr. Antonio? What's that gold thing on the front of your boat?" Ethan asked curiously.

"Every gondola has an ornament.

Mine is a . . . well, I believe the word is 'hawk' in English," Antonio replied.

"Really?" Ethan reached into his pocket and pulled out his prized gold coin from Grandpa Harry. It had a globe on one side . . . and a hawk on the other!

Huh, Ethan thought. But before he could say anything, Antonio spoke.

"Perhaps I could take you all for a ride in my gondola during your stay," he suggested. "It is hundreds of years old and used to belong to one of the doges of Venice."

"Yes, please!" Ethan and Ella said eagerly.

Maybe Venice wouldn't be such a bad place to spend a little time, after all!

A Mysterious E-mail

The next day Ella and Ethan slept way past their usual wake-up time.

"It's late!" Ethan announced from his bed across the room. "We missed breakfast!"

Ella opened her eyes and sat up in her bed. Bright sunlight streamed through the large window. A warm breeze rustled the lace curtains. Next

to her, Pumpkin stirred on the velvety green quilt, purring. The Briars had learned from Sofia that Pumpkin used to be a stray but lived at the hotel now.

Someone knocked on the door. Mr. Briar stuck his head inside. He wore jeans and a T-shirt with the red, white, and green flag of Italy on it.

"Good morning! I wanted to let you guys sleep in a bit," he said cheerfully.

"Where's Mom?" Ethan asked.

"She's at the library doing research for her column. I thought the three of us could go out for some *gelato*." Mr. Briar added, "That's the Italians' ice cream!"

Ella and Ethan laughed. Their dad *loved* trying foreign foods.

"Can I check some e-mail first?" Ella

asked. She really missed her friends back home. Maybe one of them had sent her a message.

"Yeah, me too!" Ethan said. The twins shared an e-mail address.

"Of course! My computer is on the desk," Mr. Briar replied.

Ella and Ethan hurried to the living room. Their dad's laptop sat on a fancy wooden desk with cool designs carved into it. They raced to the leather chair and scrunched onto it together.

Ethan opened their e-mail account.

There were three messages waiting for them.

The first was from Ethan's best friend, Theo, telling him about the Brookeston Boomers' soccer game against the Trumansburg Titans. The second was a message from Ella's best friend, Hannah, with a new poem she had written for their poetry club.

The third and final message was from Grandpa Harry. The subject line of his e-mail was: Two Clues.

"What does that mean? Two clues to what?" Ethan asked.

"I don't know," Ella replied. "Let's find out!"

Ethan clicked to open the e-mail from Grandpa Harry.

To: ethanella@eemail.com

From: gpaharry@eemail.com

Subject: TWO CLUES

Hello, my dears. *Benvenuti a Venezia!* (That means "Welcome to Venice!")

Venice is one of my favorite cities in the world. Your Grandma Lucy and I visited it many times when she was alive.

She and I loved the churches and the museums there. We also loved the many bridges over the canals, like the Rialto Bridge and the Bridge of Sighs. But perhaps our absolute favorite thing in Venice was a five-hundred-year-old mosaic. (A mosaic is a type of artwork made up of lots of little

pieces of glass in different colors.)

You should try to find this very special mosaic. However, it will not be easy!

I can offer you two clues to get you started:

1) Calle Farnese

2) Look up!

I know from your last mystery that you are very good at finding things. Good luck!

Lots of love,

Grandpa Harry

PS Say hello to my old friend Luigi and his son, Antonio, for me! I hope Antonio will show you his beautiful gondola, which used to belong to a doge of Venice.

Ethan glanced up from the screen. "We have to find the mosaic!" he told Ella excitedly.

"I know. But how? And who's this Calle Farnese person?" Ella said, puzzled.

"I'm not sure. Why don't you write down those clues in the notebook Grandpa Harry gave you?" Ethan suggested.

The day before their trip, Grandpa Harry had given both of the twins going-away presents.

Ethan's was the gold coin with the hawk on it. Ella's was a purple notebook. Grandpa Harry had told her that it might come in handy for solving mysteries . . . like the one they had encountered right before they left.

Ethan's coin had disappeared just hours before the Briars had to get to the airport. The twins had used Ella's notebook to keep track of clues and other information. At the last minute,

they'd found the coin in quite an unexpected place.

Now it seemed they had a *new* mystery to solve!

A Gondola Thief?

"Mmm. This is the best ice cream—I mean *gelato*—I've ever had!" Ethan said, licking his spoon.

Ella finished up the last of her *pesca* gelato. *Pesca* was Italian for "peach." "Me too!"

The twins were strolling through the crowded Piazza San Marco with their father. The piazza was an enormous

square with beautiful old buildings along the sides of it. One of the buildings was the Doge's Palace, which Mrs. Briar planned to write about.

"See that church? That's the Basilica San Marco, or St. Mark's Cathedral," Mr. Briar said, pointing. "That tall tower over there is called the Campanile di San Marco. *Campanile* means 'clock tower.' Or is it 'bell tower'? Wait. Let me check."

While Mr. Briar flipped through his guidebook, Ella scanned the crowded square. Nearby, an old man tossed bread crumbs to pigeons. With his

kind face and bushy gray hair, he reminded Ella of Grandpa Harry.

Ella pulled her purple notebook out of her pocket. She glanced at the page on which she'd written Grandpa Harry's clues about Calle Farnese and looking up. What did they mean?

"Bell tower!" Mr. Briar announced

suddenly. "The clock tower is that building, to the north. And speaking of clocks, it's almost two thirty. Let's get back to our hotel so we can dig into the wonderful world of multiplication."

Ella and Ethan groaned. With homeschooling to do, when would they find time to solve their new mystery?

Mr. Briar led the way across the piazza and onto a side street. They went over a short stone bridge.

As their dad stopped to research the name of the bridge, Ella and Ethan peered over the side. Just up the canal, a red-haired man stood on a dock next to a black and green gondola. He peered around as if to see if anyone was watching him.

Then the man jumped into the gondola and untied it from the dock. He paddled quickly away.

"What just happened?" Ethan asked Ella, puzzled.

"I don't know. Do you think he stole that gondola?" Ella said worriedly.

Ethan frowned. "It sure looked suspicious to me. . . ."

MAP OF VENICE

CHAPTER 5
Calle Farnese

When they got back to their hotel room, Mr. Briar had an important message waiting for him. He made a quick call on his cell phone, then turned to Ethan and Ella.

"Bad news," he announced. "That was the passport office. I have to go over there to straighten out a problem with our passports. I'm afraid the

wonderful world of multiplication will have to wait until later. I should be back in a few hours. Can you two find something to keep you busy while I'm gone?"

"Sure, Dad," Ella said.

"Yeah, no problem," Ethan added, trying not to smile.

Mr. Briar threw some things into a bag and left. As soon as he was gone, Ethan went over to the desk and started looking through the messy pile of books and papers.

"What are you looking for?" Ella asked him.

"A map of Venice I saw earlier," Ethan replied.

Ella put her hands on her hips. "But why?"

"Because this is our chance to sneak out and look for Grandpa Harry's mosaic!" Ethan declared. "We should go back to that bridge, too. Where

the gondola was."

Ella frowned. "Are you sure it's okay for us to go out without telling Mom and Dad anything?"

"Just trust me," Ethan assured her.

"Okay, but if we get in trouble, I'm telling them it was *your* idea," Ella insisted. While Ethan searched for the map, Ella glanced around the room. "Where's Pumpkin?"

"She's probably downstairs," Ethan

replied without looking up.

A few minutes later, Ethan found the map. It was sandwiched between two books on Italian history. He spread it out on the desk and found the Pensione Mistero on it. He marked it with a big X so they would be able to trace their way back.

Then he noticed something else. "Ella, look! Check this out!"

Ella leaned over the

map. Ethan pointed to a bunch of different streets.

They were all called Calle something. Calle de Mezo, Calle Vinanti, Calle Farnese . . .

Calle Farnese was one of the clues in Grandpa Harry's e-mail!

"Calle Farnese isn't a person. It's a street!" Ella exclaimed.

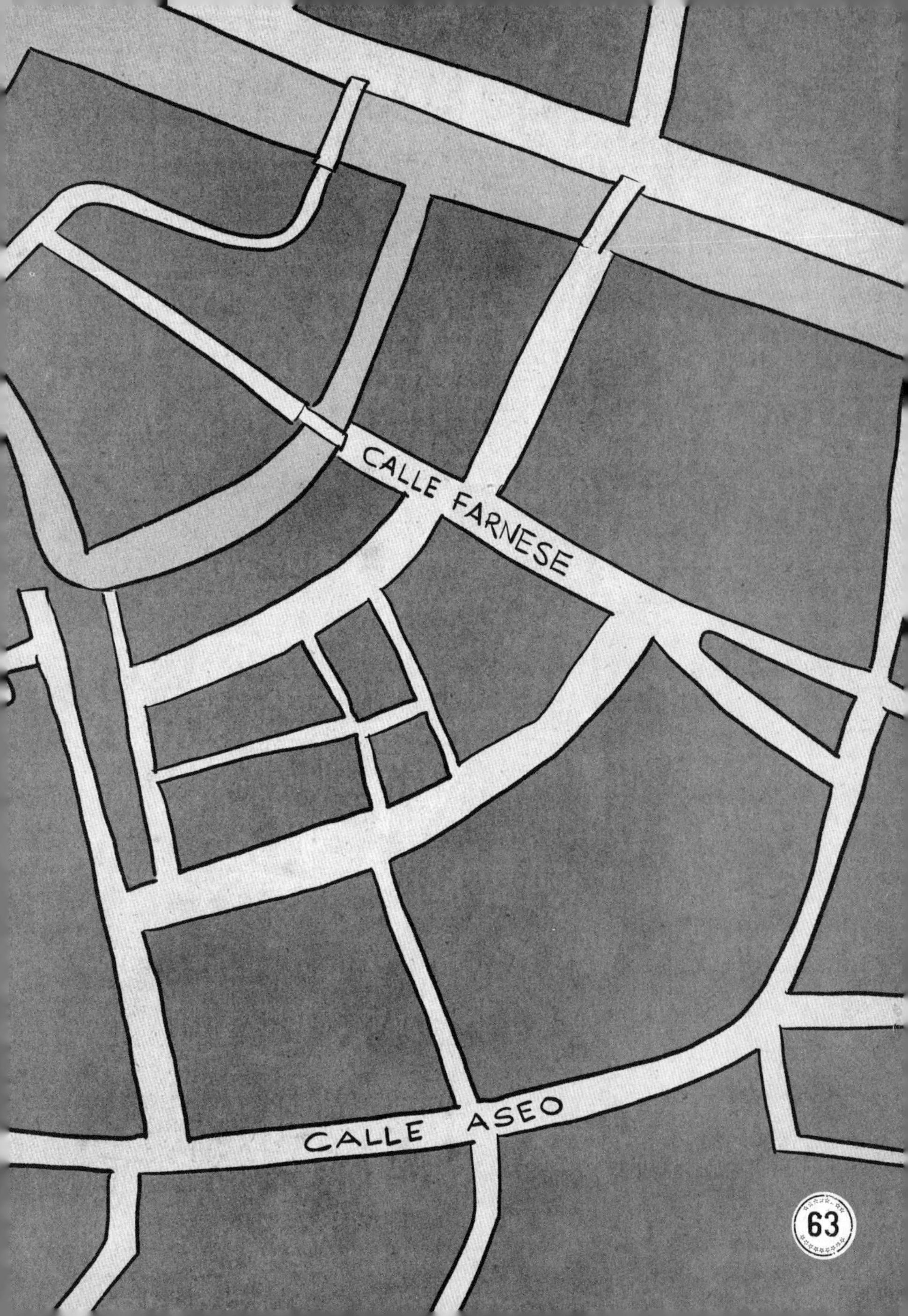
CALLE FARNESE
CALLE ASEO

Pumpkin in Trouble

"I think it's this way," Ella said, pointing to the right.

She and Ethan followed the sidewalk along the canal. Their plan was to retrace their steps back to the stone bridge, then go to Calle Farnese after that. According to the map, Calle Farnese was on the other side

of Piazza San Marco. The route there looked complicated, with lots of tiny, winding streets.

They soon reached the stone bridge. Two dark-haired men were standing at the dock where the black and green gondola had been. They seemed to be arguing.

One of the men looked familiar. "That's Antonio!" Ethan said, surprised.

The building just beyond the dock suddenly looked familiar, too. "That's the Marco Polo Ristorante!" Ella added. She hadn't recognized

the restaurant before.

Then something else clicked into place as the twins turned toward each other, wide-eyed.

The missing black and green boat must be Antonio's gondola!

Ella and Ethan rushed across the bridge and made their way over to the dock. The two men stopped arguing. "Harry Robinson's grandchildren, what are you doing here?" Antonio asked them.

"We saw someone take your boat, Mr. Antonio," Ella blurted out.

"You see? I *told* you I did not steal it," the other man said angrily to Antonio.

"I should not have jumped to conclusions, Paolo. I am very sorry," Antonio told the other man. "When

did this happen? And what did the person look like?" he asked Ella and Ethan.

"He had red hair. And we saw him take it about half an hour ago," Ethan replied.

"We must find this red-haired thief! Will you help me?" Antonio pleaded.

"We can go in my gondola," Paolo offered.

"Yes! We will take you on your very first gondola ride!" Antonio told the twins.

"Sure!" Ethan said excitedly. Ella nodded.

The four of them got into Paolo's gondola, which was tied to a nearby dock. "Which way did this man go?" Paolo asked the twins.

"Straight ahead," Ella said.

Paolo picked up an oar and began paddling. The long boat glided smoothly under the bridge and down the canal. They passed a bookstore and a bustling café. It was like riding in a canoe, but instead of being on a lake, they were in the middle of a busy city!

Ella pulled her purple notebook out of her bag and opened it to a fresh page. She got a pen out of her pocket and began writing.

A red-haired man stole Mr. Antonio's gondola.
Who is he? And why did he steal it?

Just then, Ella heard a familiar "meow." She glanced up and saw a flash of orange on the sidewalk above the canal.

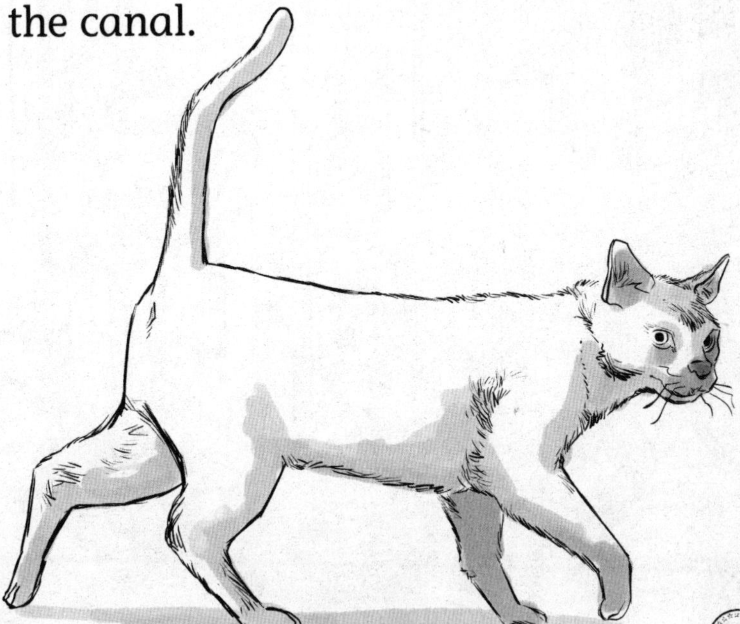

It was Pumpkin!

The little cat ran to the edge of the canal and perched over the water. She howled loudly at Ella and the others in the gondola. Suddenly, Ella saw a dog running toward Pumpkin.

"Mr. Paolo! Stop! Pumpkin is in trouble!" Ella cried out.

CHAPTER 7
Which Way?

"Pumpkin? I don't see a pumpkin," Paolo said, confused.

"That cat over there!" Ethan told him. "She lives at our hotel."

"Oh!" Paolo steered his gondola over to the sidewalk. Pumpkin jumped right in.

Ella swooped the cat up in her arms.

"I am glad we rescued little *Zucca*—I

mean, Pumpkin. But we must keep going. Otherwise we will lose our thief," Antonio said anxiously.

Paolo continued paddling down the canal. A few minutes later, they reached a fork. The canal branched off to the left and right.

Paolo turned to Antonio. "Which way do we go?"

Antonio frowned. "I am not sure. Perhaps we have lost our thief after all."

"Do you have *any* idea who that

red-haired guy might be?" Ethan asked.

Antonio shook his head.

"Who would want to steal your boat?" Ella piped up. "Do you have any enemies?"

"*Enemies?* Everyone loves Antonio!" Antonio replied.

"Maybe he stole your gondola because it belonged to that famous ruler—a *doge*," Ethan suggested.

Antonio's face lit up. He gasped. "I just remembered something! There was a man who came by to see me at the restaurant last week. He asked where I had gotten my gondola. He said that his grandfather used to own a gondola just like it, but that it was

stolen from him many years ago."
Then Antonio added, "I think the man had red hair."

"We should go talk to him!" Ella said eagerly. "Do you know his name?"

"No. But he mentioned that his wife owns a glass shop on Calle Rosanna," Antonio said.

"To Calle Rosanna now!" Paolo exclaimed, picking up his oar.

* * *

Ten minutes later, Ethan, Ella, Antonio, and Paolo reached Calle Rosanna. Laundry flapped on a clothesline that stretched from one window to another above the water. Children kicked a soccer ball on the street.

"My gondola! There it is!" Antonio shouted.

Antonio's black and green boat was docked in front of a tiny shop with a sign that said: CRISTALLERIA. Colorful figurines gleamed in the shop's window. Inside, a woman shaped a swan out of a hot,

glowing piece of molten glass. Paolo paddled over to the dock. Antonio started to climb out of Paolo's boat and into his own.

Just then, someone ran out of the shop. It was the red-haired man. And he looked angry!

CRISTALLERIA

CHAPTER 8
One More Mystery

The red-haired man began shouting in Italian. Antonio shouted back, also in Italian.

"What's happening, Mr. Paolo?" Ella asked. She held Pumpkin tightly in her arms.

"Antonio told the man—I believe his name is Carlo—to give back the gondola. Carlo said no because

the gondola rightly belongs to his grandfather," Paolo translated.

Antonio switched to English just then. "These children saw you steal my gondola!" he told Carlo, pointing to Ethan and Ella.

"You mean my *grandfather's* gondola," Carlo said angrily. "I don't know how your family came to possess it. But after I spoke to you last week, I came straight home and matched it against photographs of my grandfather's boat. They were the same. So I went to the police, but they said I had no real proof! That's why I had to take the gondola back on my own."

"How do you know the two boats are the same?" Ella asked Carlo.

Carlo was startled. "Why, because the details are identical. The black and green colors, the eagle ornament . . ."

"Wait! The ornament on this gondola is a hawk, not an eagle!" Ethan told him.

"What?" Carlo walked around to the front of the boat. He stared closely

at the ornament. Then his shoulders slumped. "You are right. It *is* a hawk ornament. I am very sorry for the confusion," he said to Antonio.

Antonio nodded. "I accept your apology," he said. "You thought you were helping your grandfather."

The two men shook hands. Then Carlo returned to the glass shop, and Antonio got into his gondola.

"*Grazie.* Thank you," Antonio said to Ethan and Ella. "If it hadn't been for you, I would never have found my boat! Now, please . . . let me take you two back to your hotel."

The twins stepped carefully into Antonio's gondola, carrying Pumpkin with them. Paolo waved and paddled off. Antonio began paddling too.

"Mr. Antonio? Can we make a quick stop first?" Ethan asked.

"*Sì!* Yes! Anything for my great

detectives!" Antonio exclaimed.

Ethan pulled the map of Venice out of his pocket. He smoothed it out on his lap and pointed to Calle Farnese. "Can you take us there? We have one more mystery to solve!" he said eagerly.

CALLE
FARNESE

CHAPTER 9
The Mosaic

"Here we are. Calle Farnese!" Antonio announced a little while later. "I will wait for you with Pumpkin while you solve your mystery. Please be careful. It is easy to get lost in Venice."

"Thank you!" Ella said.

Antonio tied the gondola to a dock. Ella and Ethan stepped out of the gondola. On the side of an old

brick building, they saw a black-and-white sign that said CALLE FARNESE. They rushed toward the sign. They were finally going to see the mosaic!

They turned onto Calle Farnese. Apartment buildings lined either side of the street, which was barely wide enough for both of them! Overhead, the twins could make out a thin sliver of blue sky.

Ethan and Ella wandered down the street, searching for the mosaic. They didn't really know where it would be. They looked at doors, through windows, and on walls. They searched all over the ground.

"How are we ever going to find it? We don't even know what it looks

like," Ethan complained.

"Grandpa said it was made up of little pieces of colored glass," Ella reminded him.

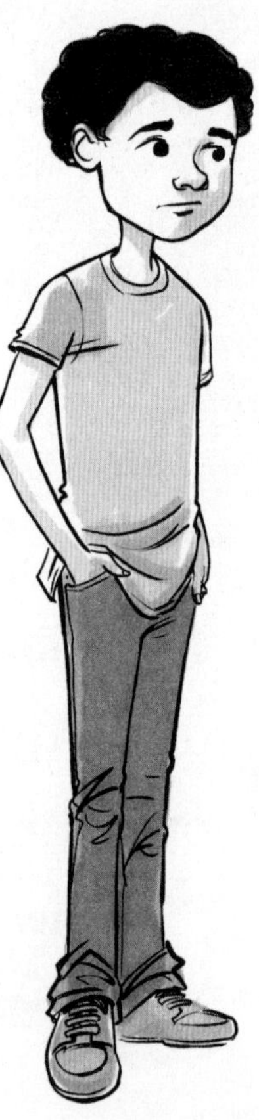

They continued down Calle Farnese, but the mosaic was nowhere in sight. After a while, they decided it was time to turn around. They had to get back to the hotel before their parents returned and realized they were missing.

"I guess we'll never

find it," Ethan said with a sigh.

"Wait! What about Grandpa's other clue?" Ella reached for her purple notebook and flipped through the pages. "Here. 'Look up.'"

The twins glanced up. But there was only sky, no mosaic.

"Look! Over there!" Ethan cried out suddenly.

Just ahead of them was a short alleyway that turned off to the left. Ella and Ethan ran over to it and tilted their heads to look up.

There it was, high on a wall!

Crafted from tiny bits of colored glass, the mosaic showed a scene of ancient Venice. A glittering glass palace stood on the banks of a glittering glass harbor. A king and queen rode on a gondola through the turquoise

glass water. An amber bird soared through the brilliant blue sky.

It was the most amazing thing they had ever seen.

CHAPTER 10

Venezia, Ti Amo

As soon as Ethan and Ella got back to their hotel with Pumpkin, they sat down at the desk to write Grandpa Harry an e-mail. Luckily, their parents were both still out. Ethan began to type.

Dear Grandpa Harry,

Guess what? We found your mosaic! My favorite part was the king. Ella says her favorite part was the sparkly blue water.

We also solved another mystery. We helped Mr. Antonio find his gondola.

Did you know that his boat has a hawk on it? Like the coin you gave me. Hawks are messengers of the sky. They're symbols of nobility, too. Nobility means you come from a rich and powerful family. We looked it up!

We decided that we love solving mysteries. And we love Venice, too! Guess how you say that in Italian? *Venezia, ti amo.*

Love,

Ethan (and Ella)

Just as Ethan hit SEND, the front door opened. Mr. and Mrs. Briar walked in.

"Look who I ran into on my way

home from the passport office!" Mr. Briar said merrily.

"I was walking back and got *so* lost." Mrs. Briar smoothed her blond hair that was tangled from the wind.

"It is very easy to get lost in Venice," Ethan said, imitating Antonio's voice.

Ella giggled.

Their parents exchanged a puzzled glance.

"So what did you kids do while we were gone?" Mrs. Briar asked.

"I hope you weren't too bored," Mr. Briar added.

"Oh no!" Ethan and Ella said at the same time.

"We weren't bored at all," Ella added.

"Good. Well, I'm afraid it's too late for our math lesson. We'll have to postpone it until tomorrow," Mr. Briar told the twins. "Your mom and I had a great idea, though. Why don't we go for your very first gondola ride? We know you kids were excited about that."

Ethan and Ella smiled at each other. It would be their *second* very first gondola ride in Venice!

GLOSSARY

basilica = cathedral

Benvenuti = Welcome

Buon giorno = Good day

Buona sera = Good evening

calle = street

campanile = bell tower

cristalleria = glassware

Grazie = Thank you

pesca = peach
ristorante = restaurant
Sì = yes
Ti amo = I love you
Venezia = Venice
zucca = pumpkin

*All words are in Italian.

Ella Briar gazed out the airplane window. Below, miles of glittering lights twinkled against the evening sky. “Look, Ethan!” she said to her twin.

“That must be Paris,” Ethan replied. “It’s awesome!”

"I think that's the Eiffel Tower," Ella said, pointing.

"Did you know that the Eiffel Tower is the tallest structure in Paris?" their dad, Andrew, called out from across the aisle. "It was built in 1889 for the world's fair."

"I see a river!" Ethan announced.

"Probably the Seine," Mr. Briar guessed. "It divides Paris into two parts, the Right Bank and the Left Bank."

"We're staying in a lovely old neighborhood on the Right Bank," their mom, Josephine, said as she smoothed on lipstick. "There are a lot of fun shops there! *And* we'll be close to a famous museum called the Louvre."

Fun shops? A famous museum? The twins couldn't wait!

A short while later, their plane landed at the airport. The Briars took a taxi to the apartment they were renting. The building had no elevator, so they had to carry their suitcases up five flights of marble stairs. They were out of breath by the time they got to the top.

The climb was worth it, though. The apartment was enormous, with an elegant balcony that overlooked red rooftops and bustling cafés. Brightly lit boats cruised along the river. In the distance, the Eiffel Tower shimmered like a gold jewel.

Ella remembered from her dad's guidebook that Paris was often called the City of Light. Now she knew why!

Ethan ran straight to the biggest bedroom. "Dibs!" he shouted.

"Hey, not fair!" Ella protested.

"How about your father and I take this room?" Mrs. Briar suggested. "Ethan, there's a green room down the hall with soccer posters. And, Ella, the purple room has lots of books in English."

Ella loved books, and purple was her favorite color! She raced down the hallway with her suitcase and found her room. It had a canopy bed with a lavender bedspread. Black-and-white photographs of Paris covered the walls.

Next to the bed was a wooden bookshelf. Ella spotted a couple of books she'd already read, *The Phantom Tollbooth* and *Matilda*. Tucked between them was a dusty old volume called *Les Secrets de Paris*.

Curious, she picked it up and flipped to the first page. It was all in French. However, someone had scribbled something in English: "Paris is full of secret places that you will not find in any guidebook."

Ella shivered with excitement. What did that mean? Would she and Ethan stumble upon any of these secret places while *they* were in Paris?